Cat Jokes

Johnny B. Laughing

DEDICATION

This book is dedicated to everyone that loves a funny joke. Laughter is one of the best gifts you can give. It always puts a smile on your face, warms your heart, and makes you feel great.

CONTENTS

FUNNY CAT JOKES

Q: What do you call a cat when he first wakes up with the alarm clock?

A: Catsup!

Q: Why do cats eat fur balls?

A: Because they love a good gag!

Q: What do you call it when a cat stops?

A: A paws!

Q: Why did the mother cat put stamps on her kittens?

A: Because she wanted to mail a litter.

Q: How do cats buy things?

A: From a cat-alogue!

Q: What kind of cats lay around the house?

A: Car-pets!

Q: What kind of work does a weak cat do?

A: Light mouse work.

Q: What's a cat's second favorite food?

A: Spa-catti!

Q: What's a cat's favorite food?

A: Petatoes!

Q: Which game did the cat want to play with the mouse?

A: Catch.

Q: What do you call a cat that's joined the Red Cross?

A: A first-aid kit!

Q: What do you call a cat that eats lemons?

A: A sourpuss!

Q: Why does everyone love cats?

A: They are the purr-fect pet!

Q: Where do cats write down notes?

A: Scratch Paper!

Q: What's every cat's favorite song?

A: Three Blind Mice!

Q: Why do cats like to hear other cats make noise?

A: It's meow-sic to their ears!

Q: What did the female cat say to the male cat?

A: You're a purr-fect cat for me!

This is Sus

Q: What do you call it when a cat bites?

A: Catnip!

Q: What do cats like to eat on a hot day?

A: Mice cream

Q: What do you call the loser in a hissing, scratching cat fight?

A: Claude.

Q: What has one horn and gives milk?

A: A milk truck.

Q: Why couldn't the cat speak?

A: The dog taped his mouth.

Q: If a cat won an Oscar, what would he get?

A: An a-CAT-emy award.

Q: Why was the cat afraid of the tree?

A: Because of the tree bark.

Q: What is an octopus?

A: An eight-sided cat.

Q: What is another way to describe a cat?

A: A heat seeking missile!

Q: Why was the cat so small?

A: Because it only had condensed milk!

Q: When the cats away..?

A: The house smells better!

Q: Which big cat should you never play cards with?

A: A cheetah!

Q: Why are cats such good singers?

A: They're very mewsical.

Q: What do you call a cat that can spring up a six-foot wall?

A: A good jumpurr!

Q: What's furry, has whiskers, and chases outlaws?

A: A posse cat!

Q: What is a cat's favorite TV show?

A: Miami Mice!

Q: What did the cat say to the fish?

A: I've got a bone to pick with you!

Q: Why do cats never shave?

A: Because 8 out of 10 cats prefer whiskas!

Q: When is it unlucky to see a black cat?

A: When you're a mouse!

Q: Why did the cat sleep under the car?

A: Because she wanted to wake up oily!

Q: What happened when the cat swallowed a coin?

A: There was some money in the kitty!

Q: What did the cat do when he swallowed some cheese?

A: He waited by the mouse hole with baited breath!

Q: What does a cat call a bowl of mice?

A: A purrfect meal!

Q: What do you call a cat wearing boots?

A: Puss in boots!

Q: What works in a circus, walks a tightrope, and has claws?

A: An acrocat!

Q: Why did the cat put the letter M into the fridge?

A: Because it turns ice into mice!

Q: What cat purrs more than any other?

A: Purrsians!

Q: On what should you mount a statue of your cat?

A: A caterpillar!

Q: What do cats read in the morning?

A: Mewspapers!

Q: Why do cats chase birds?

A: For a lark!

Q: What kind of cat should you take into the desert?

A: A first aid kitty!

Q: What do you call a cat that has just eaten a whole duck?

A: A duck filled fatty puss!

Q: Why do tomcats fight?

A: Because they like raising a stink!

Q: What is white, sugary, has whiskers, and floats on the sea?

A: A catameringue!

Q: There were four cats in a boat, one jumped out. How many were left?

A: None. They were all copy cats!

Q: What do you get if you cross a cat with Father Christmas?

A: Santa Claws!

Q: How do you know that cats are not sensitive creatures?

A: They never cry over spilt milk!

Q: What is cleverer than a talking cat?

A: A spelling bee!

Q: Who was the most powerful cat in China?

A: Chairman Miaow!

Q: What do you get if you cross a cat with a tree?

A: A cat-a-logue!

Q: What's the unluckiest kind of cat to have?

A: A catastrophe!

Q: What noise does a cat make going down the highway?

A: Miaooooooooooooooooooooooooooooow!

Q: How is cat food sold?

A: Usually purr can!

Q: What is the cat's favorite TV show?

A: The evening mews!

Q: What do you get if you cross a cat and a gorilla?

A: An animal that puts you out a night!

Q: How do you know if your cat has eaten a duckling?

A: She's got that down in the mouth look!

Q: How do you know if you cats got a bad cold?

A: He has cat-arrh!

Q: What did the cat say when he lost all his money?

A: I'm paw!

Q: How do cats eat spaghetti?

A: The same as everyone else - they put it in their mouths!

Q: What do you get if you cross a cat with a parrot?

A: A carrot!

Q: What happened when the cat ate a ball of wool?

A: She had mittens!

HOW MANY CATS?

FIND THE DIFFERENCES

FIND
10
DIFFERENCES

MAZE #1

MAZE #2

MAZE #3

MAZE #4

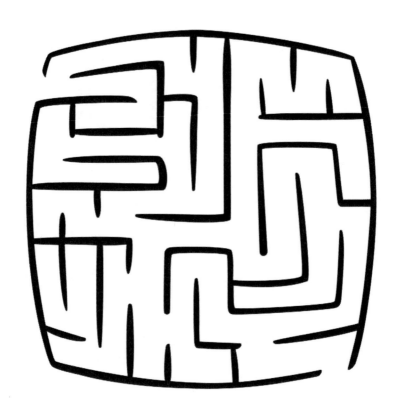

MAZE #5

HOW MANY CATS SOLUTION

FIND THE DIFFERENCES SOLUTION

MAZE SOLUTIONS

ABOUT THE AUTHOR

The Joke King, Johnny B. Laughing is a best-selling children's joke book author. He is a jokester at heart and enjoys a good laugh, pulling pranks on his friends, and telling funny and hilarious jokes!

For more funny joke books just search for JOHNNY B. LAUGHING on Amazon

-or-

Visit the website:
www.funny-jokes-online.weebly.com

Made in United States
North Haven, CT
26 July 2022

21859906R00020